Cleopatra

Adèle Geras
Illustrated by M. P. Robertson

KINGFISHER
NEW YORK

This one is for
Guy Henry Jones
A. G.

Thanks to Jenny (Cleo)
and Ellie (Nefret)
M. P. R.

KINGFISHER
LONDON & NEW YORK

Copyright © Kingfisher 2007
Text copyright © Adèle Geras 2007
Illustration copyright © M. P. Robertson 2007
Published in the United States by Kingfisher,
175 Fifth Ave., New York, NY 10010
Kingfisher is an imprint of Macmillan Children's Books, London.
All rights reserved.

Distributed in the U.S. by Macmillan, 175 Fifth Ave.,
New York, NY 10010

LIBRARY OF CONGRESS CATALOGING-IN-PUBLICATION DATA
Geras, Adèle.
  Cleopatra / Adèle Geras.—1st ed.
    p. cm.
  Includes index.
  1. Cleopatra, Queen of Egypt, d. 30 B.C.—Juvenile literature. 2.
Egypt—History—332-30 B.C.—Juvenile literature. 3. Queens—
Egypt—Biography—Juvenile literature. I. Title.
  DT92.7.G47 2007
  932'.021092—dc22
  [B]
                                    2006102066

ISBN 978-0-7534-6673-5

Kingfisher books are available for special promotions and premiums.
For details contact: Special Markets Department, Macmillan,
175 Fifth Ave., New York, NY 10010.

For more information, please visit www.kingfisherbooks.com

Printed in China
10 9 8 7 6 5 4 3 2 1
ITR/0511/LFG/SCHOY(SCHOY)/140MA

Contents

Nefret's Diary

Nefret's diary entries tell about events that happened between the years we now call 41–40 B.C. She also refers to historical events— such as the civil war between Roman generals Julius Caesar and Pompey—that happened as far back as 49 B.C. Nefret could not have known these dates, so they are not used in her diary extracts. Like most ordinary people in Egypt, Nefret did not use a calendar or give names to the months. A calendar was used for official business, by scientists and scribes and other important people.

Before Sunset

THIRD MONTH. FIVE DAYS BEFORE THE FULL MOON.

My name is Nefret, which means "pretty." My mother says that I'm lucky, too. That's because I can read and write. My friend Rami, who is the son of one of the palace scribes, taught me everything he learned. This means that I can write down all of the important things that happen to me. Rami has given me some papyrus scrolls to use as a diary, and I will start writing now, because I have so much to tell. At the next full moon, when I'm ten, I will be going to work for Queen Cleopatra at the royal palace. I can't wait to live in the palace! Both of my brothers have grown up and left home, but my little sister, Kebi, shares a sleeping mat with me. She kicks me at night. It will be wonderful to have a mat all to myself.

The women in our family have always worked for the royal household. I hope that when the time comes for me to leave my mother's house, Lotus Blossom, my beautiful, green-eyed cat, can come with me. She sits beside me as I write and looks down at the papyrus as if she's reading a story.

Nefret's mother

Nefret

Lotus Blossom

Kebi, Nefret's sister

I live in Egypt—in Alexandria, a port that's always crowded with ships from all over the Mediterranean Sea. The royal family's house is here too. It's a splendid palace guarded by soldiers. Behind the palace are the small houses where the servants of the royal household, including my parents and Rami's parents, live.

Our river, the Nile, floods the surrounding plains once each year, and then there's enough wheat and barley to feed all of the people. In the temples devoted to our gods, we offer prayers that the river may continue to give us all the food that we need. In years when the floods don't come, the people starve, and there's almost no grain in the huge grain stores.

Lotus meows very loudly when she's hungry, but there always seems to be mice around for her to catch, so she'll be all right. I just hope that there's enough food in the palace for me!

When the Nile river floods, there is a good harvest and plenty of grain for everyone.

Rami isn't my only friend. I have many companions. My best girlfriends are Nanu and Sheriti. They help me take care of Kebi sometimes. We play games and go swimming and take part in gymnastic competitions. Kebi likes those the best, because she's better at running and jumping than I am. But I'm a stronger swimmer, and Kebi doesn't even know how to write her name! I hope that some of my friends will come to work in the palace when I do, or who will I play with when my work is done?

Alexandria is a busy port on the Mediterranean Sea. Hundreds of merchant traders from different countries visit, and many languages are spoken in the marketplace.

My mother has told me many things about Queen Cleopatra. I have decided to write them all down in this diary before I go to work at the palace. Then, when I meet the queen, she will be amazed that I already seem to know her!

I know that the queen is not exactly beautiful, but she's so charming that everyone who meets her thinks that she is the loveliest person they've ever seen. Her smile is enchanting, and so is her voice. She's very intelligent and can speak nine languages. I can only speak Egyptian and a little bit of Cat, which is useful when I'm talking to Lotus.

Here's what else I know. The queen's family was from Macedonia, but she was born in Egypt and wants to make us as powerful as the Romans. My mother says that she had a great struggle to become our queen, overcoming many enemies to do so. She was only 17 when she came to the throne. She wasn't allowed to rule on her own, but had to have a husband, so she married one of her younger brothers, Ptolemy. My mother said that it was a marriage in name only, which means that she didn't have to kiss her brother or anything like that. If I had to marry one of my brothers, I'd run away forever!

The queen's brother-husband, Ptolemy, had some scheming advisers who plotted against Cleopatra.

Ptolemy was much younger than Cleopatra, so she was the real ruler. But Ptolemy didn't like the idea of not being in charge. He didn't like being bossed around by his sister, and he had some sly men to advise him. These advisers of Ptolemy were old men, and they hated Cleopatra being the queen. They were always plotting against her.

Cleopatra had trouble with the Romans, too. The Roman Empire was enormous, and because there were so many men in the Roman legions, feeding and paying them all was a problem. The Romans were always trying to get ahold of Egypt's grain and jewels and gold. Two important Roman generals were fighting each other. They were named Julius Caesar and Pompey. Julius Caesar won a big sea battle in Pharsalus, so Pompey fled to Alexandria, thinking that young Ptolemy would protect him.

Pompey

Julius Caesar

I must stop writing now. It's time for my dancing lesson. I love dancing, and this is my favorite lesson of all. I will see Nanu and Sheriti, but first I must find the dress that I have to wear. Perhaps Kebi has hidden it? She does this sometimes, and then I get so annoyed that I say I'll pull her hair. She hates having her hair pulled, so she always tells me where it is right away.

Just After Dawn
THIRD MONTH. FOUR DAYS BEFORE THE FULL MOON.

I am writing this before the morning meal. Lotus woke me up by jumping on my pillow and leaving a few feathers there. Ugh! She's been chasing birds . . . they're her favorite early-morning snack.

Now I can't fall back to sleep. My mother didn't want to tell me about the death of the Roman general Pompey, because she thought that it might give me nightmares. But I asked Rami, and he told me what happened. He knows a lot of things. Our families have arranged for us to get married, but that's not for years yet, when I'm almost 13. I won't mind marrying him. He's always nice to me.

Rami told me that horrible young Ptolemy gave orders to his men to kill Pompey.

Ptolemy wanted to please Julius Caesar. He thought that Caesar would like to see the head of his enemy brought to him in a straw basket. He was wrong. Caesar was furious and also very sad, because Pompey used to be one of his allies. Julius Caesar ordered Ptolemy and Cleopatra to come to see him.

Julius Caesar was horrified when he realized what Ptolemy had done.

Cleopatra arranged for her trusted bodyguard to deliver a very special rug to the palace.

My mother told me what happened next. She said that Cleopatra wanted to see Julius Caesar without Ptolemy so that she could tell him that her little brother was not to be trusted. She arranged for a boat to be rowed to the palace jetty, and in that boat was a rolled-up rug. The oarsman shouted up to the guards, "Hey, there's a delivery here for Julius Caesar. One very beautiful Oriental rug. It's urgent."

No one asked why the rug had to be delivered so urgently. They probably thought that if Caesar had ordered it, he'd want it brought to him at once. So they opened the gate, and the man in the boat lifted the rolled-up rug onto his shoulder. When he reached the room that Caesar was in, he lowered the rug to the ground and let it unroll across the marble floor. "And guess what happened next?" my mother asked when she told me the story. I couldn't guess. When she told me, I laughed so much that Lotus jumped off my lap and went to hide behind a screen.

Cleopatra had to be smuggled into Caesar's room because she did not trust Ptolemy or his advisers.

Cleopatra had been rolled up in the rug the whole time! As soon as it was unrolled, she jumped out and smiled at Julius Caesar. And when he saw her, he fell in love with her. My mother says that Cleopatra has a magic about her that makes every man who sees her fall in love with her.

Now it's time to put away my writing material for today. My mother has gone to prepare the morning meal. Lotus knows that there will be milk for her, and I can smell the bread baking.

Before Sunset
THIRD MONTH. TWO DAYS BEFORE THE FULL MOON.

Cleopatra's name as a "cartouche," written in Egyptian hieroglyphics by Rami.

Rami has just shown me how to write the queen's name in the picture writing that the scribes use. I feel very smart! I copied what he showed me so well that he praised me for my work.

When Rami left, I went to find my mother. I asked her to finish telling me about Cleopatra and Julius Caesar, because the day after my birthday I'm moving to the palace. Sometimes I feel excited about this, but I'm also a little nervous. The queen's husband was found drowned in the Nile river. Did she and Caesar plot to kill him? If the queen can have her own brother killed, what might she do to a maidservant?

My mother told me that everyone knew that Julius Caesar and Queen Cleopatra were in love. But it wasn't just love that made them take a long trip down the Nile river. They wanted to be seen together by the Egyptian people—the queen of Egypt and one of the rulers of Rome. I was much younger then, but I do remember my mother taking me to the port to see them leave.

"Nefret," my mother said, "the royal barge had never looked as fine as this before. It was specially decorated for the voyage. The cabins were filled with servants and food and wine. Musicians played beautiful music, while Cleopatra and Caesar lay on pillows. They wanted to show everyone in the country how powerful the queen was and how friendly she was with the most powerful man in Rome."

I thought it sounded like a kind of vacation, and I pictured them spending hours staring into each other's eyes, curled up together, just like me and Lotus. I'd love to go sailing down the river, but Lotus would hate it. She does not like getting her fur wet!

I listened intently as my mother continued. "On Cleopatra and Julius Caesar's trip, the river was in flood, and all you could see in some places was water from the ship to the horizon." My mother said that when they reached the temple of the goddess Isis in Philae, they sailed between the columns by candlelight.

Everyone knows that the queen is the goddess Isis on Earth. They say that she sometimes puts on clothes like the ones that the goddess wears in the many pictures of her that decorate the walls of the palace. These garments are made of gold. She wears a feather cape around her shoulders, and every feather is painted with liquid gold leaf.

Egyptians believe that as the queen, Cleopatra is the goddess Isis come down to Earth.

Cleopatra's ten-year-old brother-husband liked having the protection of the Roman soldiers.

"A short while after their trip," my mother continued, "Julius Caesar went back to Rome. But he left three legions of Roman soldiers behind to protect Cleopatra . . . and to protect Rome's interest in Egypt. Cleopatra still had to have a husband, so she married her other little brother, also named Ptolemy, and he was only ten years old!"

While Caesar was away, the queen gave birth to Caesar's son, Ptolemy-Caesar, known as Caesarion. She thought that their child would be able to reign over Egypt and also rule the Roman Empire when he grew up.

Cleopatra missed Julius Caesar so much that she followed him to Rome. She stayed there for two years, and Caesar gave her money and treasures of all kinds. She lived in great luxury, and there was even a statue dedicated to her in the Temple of Venus.

Julius Caesar was murdered on a day people called the "ides of March."

But not everyone was happy. The Romans didn't think that their leader should be so friendly with an Egyptian queen. They didn't want Caesar thinking that he was a king. They were worried too that the power of the Roman Empire might pass to an Egyptian.

Then a terrible thing happened. On the 14th day of the third month, Caesar was brutally stabbed to death by his enemies.

My mother said that Queen Cleopatra was so frightened of what might happen without Caesar to protect her that she decided to come home to Egypt.

So that's why she needs more servants to work for her, and one of them is going to be me! I wonder if I'll have to care for her little boy? I don't think that I'd like that very much. I remember Kebi when she was two years old. She used to cry a lot and sometimes smelled. Cats are much cleaner, and they always sleep soundly.

Sunset
THIRD MONTH. FULL MOON.

Music and dancing are an important part of every celebration. Girls usually dance in pairs—and never with boys—and dances include acrobatics.

We've been celebrating my tenth birthday. My mother made so much food! And all of my relatives came to visit us and join in the feast. It was good to see my brothers again. All of my friends have given me gifts: carved wooden animals and charms to hang on the necklace that my parents gave me. The dancing master arranged a dance in my honor, and all of my friends took part in the display. It has been a wonderful time.

Tomorrow morning, I will go with my mother to the palace. I must take my papyrus scrolls with me, but I don't know if I will find time to write about my life in the palace. Lotus is coming with me, because the queen loves cats! I hope that there are still many soldiers to protect the queen at the palace. Lotus isn't a very good guard cat. She'd be very scared if anyone came banging on the doors.

Early Morning
FIFTH MONTH. THREE-QUARTER MOON.

I've been living at the palace for almost two months. There has been too much to learn, and I haven't been able to find a quiet time to write till now.

When I first arrived at the palace, I thought that the queen would be too unhappy to talk to me. She still must have been so sad about Julius Caesar. Then her other brother-husband died, and people were saying that he'd been poisoned. But she was very kind to me.

"Nefret," she said, "you are worthy of your name. Welcome to my palace. And you have a cat, I'm told, who's

coming to live here too. What's her name?"

"Lotus Blossom, my lady. I call her Lotus."

"She's welcome too. My beloved Topaz will be happy to have a friend. He was lonely while we were away in Rome."

As soon as I heard Cleopatra speak, I knew that I'd do anything she asked of me. Her voice was like the sweetest music, and I felt happy when I listened to it.

My duties are to attend to the queen at ceremonial occasions, and I take care of her night garments. I have to see that they are taken to the washerwomen and returned to the chest, where I scatter them with fragrant herbs. Sometimes I'm in the chamber when the queen gets dressed. I have never seen such fine clothes as Cleopatra has in her sandalwood chests. There is fine-spun wool dyed in rich colors. There is linen, too, and everything is decorated by the fine stitching of the palace embroiderers, who sew pretty pictures and patterns around the hems and sleeves of every dress.

Cleopatra's favorite bracelet is in the form of a gold snake that winds up her arm.

Her golden Isis costume has a chest of its own. Every headdress that Cleopatra owns is put away in a box when she has finished wearing it. Each one is studded with gemstones the size of small onions and sewn with gold and silver coins that glitter as the queen passes by. On all of the gold coins that are used to buy and sell things in Egypt, she is dressed as Isis, and her son Caesarion is shown as the god Horus.

She has carved wooden chests overflowing with necklaces, brooches, jewel-encrusted headbands, and bracelets. Corals from the seabed make her necklaces; moonstones from the desert glow in her rings. Her bed is decorated with paintings of water lilies and cats and hawks. The snake, sacred to Isis, is her favorite creature, and she has a gold bracelet in the shape of an asp that winds all the way up her arm.

On ceremonial occasions, Cleopatra dresses as the goddess Isis; her son Caesarion dresses as the god Horus.

As well as always being careful to appear in her finest robes and most precious stones, Cleopatra also reads a lot and studies many things.

The queen spends most of her time in the library, learning about the world and all of the marvels that may be found in it. She reads scrolls about science, astrology, and history. She also knows how to calculate numbers and how to decipher codes and strange languages. I'd love to be as intelligent as her.

Cleopatra is well known for her intelligence. She reads a lot and can speak nine languages.

Afternoon

SEVENTH MONTH. TWO DAYS BEFORE THE FULL MOON.

Last night I was too nervous to sleep. I, Nefret, had been chosen by the queen to be a handmaid on a journey that she was making to Tarsus. She was going to the camp of Mark Antony, one of the rulers of the Roman Empire. I'd been told that he wanted to make sure that Cleopatra had not ganged up against him by forming an alliance with his enemies.

"Nefret," the queen said to me, "you must come with me on this voyage. You're my prettiest handmaid. Everyone on the banks will stare at us as we pass, and when Mark

Antony sees my barge in all of its splendor, he'll be dazzled by the sight, I promise you."

The royal barge is loaded with food and drinks for the journey to Tarsus.

Early Morning
SEVENTH MONTH. FULL MOON.

The day before we set sail was so busy. All of the cooks and serving women made many trips to and from the kitchens, bringing all of the food and drinks that we were going to need onto the royal barge. I was feeling nervous before we set off. Waving goodbye to my mother and Kebi made me wish that they were coming too. Lotus wasn't there to say goodbye, but I knew that she would miss me and that I would long for her company too. But the barge was so splendid!

The sails of our vessel were cut from purple silk, and three men had worked for days painting the high stern with fresh gold leaf. I was one of six handmaids, and we were dressed as mermaids in sea-green jeweled robes.

Our hair had been braided with silver thread. My dress fit me as tightly as another skin, and as the sun shone on us during the journey, I grew more and more uncomfortable. But I held myself very straight and remembered to smile, as the queen herself had instructed. Musicians played their flutes as we sailed up the river. The melodies floated over the water, and the sailors bent their oars to the rhythm.

Cleopatra, dressed up as the goddess Aphrodite, was wearing a robe made of such delicate fabric that her perfect figure could be seen through the embroidered cloth. She lay on a couch piled with silken pillows, and young boys dressed as cupids fanned her with enormous peacock-feather fans.

Men have worked for days getting the ship ready for the journey.

Many people had gathered on the
riverbank to stare at the queen as our ship
sailed toward Tarsus, but there was no sign
of Mark Antony. Cleopatra was determined
that he would come to her. She was a queen
and also a goddess. She wasn't going to
leave her ship to go to see him, even if he
was one of the most powerful men in Rome.
She had wanted him to come to Egypt
to see her, but he wouldn't. So she
decided that the ship that she was on was
part of her kingdom, because *she* was on
it. The ship, she said, is Egypt, so that's
where he had to come! People don't like to
cross the queen when she's in this kind of
mood. They also remember what
happened to her brothers.

In the end, Mark Antony came down
to the water's edge and then onto the
barge to dine with Cleopatra. I wonder
whether he's going to fall in love with
her, just like Julius Caesar did.

Early Morning
SEVENTH MONTH.   THIRD DAY AFTER THE FULL MOON.

Many people think that Cleopatra is too extravagant. But the Romans love good food, and Cleopatra needs them on her side.

I had never seen such a banquet! Thousands of rushlights flickered in every part of the ship and were reflected in the black water of the river. The palace cooks were famous, and Mark Antony ate and drank as he had never eaten and drunk before. I heard him say so, for I was near him, trying to stop the naughty boys who were dressed as cupids from helping themselves to the food. There were stuffed, roasted boars, peacocks that had been cooked and then decorated with their own gorgeous tail feathers spread out, mountains of fruit glazed with sugar, and cakes soaked in honey.

At the end of this meal, Cleopatra took one of her pearl earrings and dropped it into her goblet. Then she drank down the wine quickly, and Mark Antony's eyes opened wide to see such extravagance: imagine thinking so little of a precious pearl that you would swallow it! It was obvious that our queen had impressed him. She must be wealthy beyond his wildest dreams and also as bewitching as everyone said she was. He couldn't stop looking at her. When Mark Antony and Cleopatra had finished eating, I was dismissed, together with all of the other servants. Cleopatra was alone with him at last.

I went to where the mats were laid out for the handmaids. I was the youngest, and the others were very nice to me. When I lay down, I thought of Lotus going to sleep on some other mat in the palace. Maybe she'd been having her own little banquet of mice.

Cleopatra is determined to win Mark Antony's heart in order to protect Egypt. She is using all of her powers to woo him.

Very Early Morning
Eighth Month. Waning Moon.

We are still in Tarsus. I'm beginning to wonder when we are going to return to Alexandria, as I am missing my family and Lotus.

Mark Antony invited the queen to a banquet in his camp, and this time she accepted. The older handmaids said that Mark Antony was determined to give Queen Cleopatra an even better feast than the one that she had organized for him. All of the queen's handmaids attended her, but we did not have to wear our mermaid robes. I'm glad, because mine was so tight and hot.

Mark Antony was very loud and rude all evening. He told a lot of disgusting jokes, but the queen laughed at them—she must really like him! Everyone was lying down to eat. They rested on one elbow and used the other arm to reach for their food and drinks. They even fed each other by dangling things like grapes over each other's mouths. My mother would not be happy to see this. She makes us sit down on the floor, cross-legged, and eat with both hands. But some of the food did look delicious—although nothing could be as wonderful as the banquet that we had on the royal barge.

We didn't get back to the boat until almost sunrise! I could hardly keep my eyes open, but when we got back, I still had to help with the queen's clothing. Tomorrow we are going to return to Alexandria. I'm longing to see my mother and sister and all of my friends, especially Rami. They might even be a little envious of me. I hope that Lotus remembers me.

Mark Antony wants to show Cleopatra that the Romans can entertain too.

Morning
ELEVENTH MONTH. HALF-MOON.

Mark Antony hasn't gone back to Rome! He is spending the whole winter with Cleopatra in Alexandria.

We've been back in Alexandria for a while now, and I've had so much to tell my mother. Lotus must have missed me, because she follows me everywhere and even wanted to curl up on this papyrus, but I chased her off. She's now sulking on a pillow by my elbow, so I can write freely.

The queen brought Mark Antony back with us to Egypt, even though he has a wife in Rome! My mother shrugged her shoulders yesterday when I visited and told her the news. "She's an enchantress. I've always told you so. There isn't a man alive who doesn't fall under her spell."

Some royal servants do not approve of the queen's behavior with Mark Antony.

My mother was right. The queen and Mark Antony are deeply in love. Everyone in the palace can see that. They do everything together: riding, hunting, eating, drinking, and even going around the city in disguise, playing tricks on unsuspecting people! The older servants never stop tutting and sighing, but there isn't anything that they can do to stop it. Cleopatra always does exactly what she wants to do. I haven't told anyone this, but yesterday I heard someone whispering that the queen is expecting another baby. I wonder what Caesarion will think about having a little brother or sister. I love my sister, even though she was often a pest when she was younger.

Before the Morning Meal
TWELFTH MONTH. THREE-QUARTER MOON.

Today the queen has decided that she wants to go with Mark Antony to watch him exercising his troops. I wonder what the Roman soldiers will think about that.

All of her servants had to rise early to make sure that she was dressed for the outdoors and that her makeup was just right for the hot sun. The palace cooks were busy again, preparing food for the day. One of the older servants told me that Mark Antony has a huge army—and that many of its legions are here in Egypt.

Although he is a Roman general, Mark Antony keeps part of his army in Egypt.

I don't understand it. How can Mark Antony be living in Egypt with Cleopatra, when he is one of the rulers of another country? I am going to ask Rami if he can try to explain it to me. His father, as a scribe, will know all about it because he has to write all of the official messages for the queen.

Now that Cleopatra has departed for the day, I can have my morning meal, and so can Lotus Blossom, who always seems to be hungry. Then we can go to find Rami—I hope that he will have time to spend with me today.

Just Before Sunset
FIRST MONTH. FULL MOON.

Rami has told me what he knows about Mark Antony and Rome. He said that Mark Antony rules the Roman Empire with two other men, Octavian and Lepidus. But while Mark Antony is in Egypt, Octavian thinks that he is the real ruler—especially because his uncle was the great Roman general Julius Caesar. Octavian wants to be the most powerful man in Rome, so Mark Antony's wife, Fulvia, is trying to protect her husband's interests while he's away. I wonder if she knows that her husband is in love with Cleopatra. I don't think that I would be so nice to Rami if he decided to move away from me.

Life at the palace is never dull. Visitors come from all over the world, and rooms for them have to be prepared. In the evenings, when guests are in the palace, the queen fills the halls with music makers who play flutes and drums and pipes, and there are dancers to entertain her friends. I sometimes stand behind a pillar and watch the festivities. One night, Cleopatra ordered the palace cooks to roast 12 pigs, but at different times. This was so that one of the pigs would be ready whenever Mark Antony wanted it. How the cooks feasted that night on the food that was left over! I think that they must have given Lotus some scraps, because she is getting fat!

The cooks roasted 12 pigs at different times so that Mark Antony could eat when he wanted.

Just After Sunrise
SECOND MONTH. QUARTER MOON.

The queen is furious. A messenger came for Mark Antony yesterday, saying that he must return to Rome because Fulvia needs his help to fight off Octavian. We could all hear Cleopatra shouting at Mark Antony. "But what about me? I need you here. I am the queen of Egypt, and I demand that you stay with me." But he has left, and we are all very nervous about what might happen . . .

After the Midday Meal
SECOND MONTH. HALF-MOON.

The queen is no longer furious. She has heard that Mark Antony's wife died before he got back to Rome. Cleopatra is happy, because he will be free to marry her, and they can rule Rome and Egypt together! Now she is calling me to dress her up as the goddess Aphrodite. She wants to look beautiful when Mark Antony returns. Since the trip to Tarsus, I have been taking care of the queen's jewelry, which is a big responsibility. I also have to make sure that the salves and ointments that she uses on her face are always clean and ready to use.

There are red ointments to make her lips shine and black kohl with which she draws lines around her eyes. Her hair oil, which is made from crushed coconuts, is kept in glass bottles, and these have to be kept very clean. Her perfumes are kept in pottery vials so that the light will not reach them and spoil them. Cleopatra smells like sandalwood and cypress wood and crushed roses. You can always tell when she's been in a room.

The queen's happiness did not last long. Another messenger came from Rome with bad news. I heard the queen asking him whether he was sure and whether he'd gotten the message right. But he had. Mark Antony is not coming back. He has to stay in Rome, and, even worse, he has married someone else. His new wife is Octavia, Octavian's sister. Cleopatra knows that Antony does not love Octavia—it's just one of those "marriages of convenience" that my mother told me about. But it means that he won't be with Cleopatra when her baby is born. How sad for her.

All of her servants are going to try to cheer her up. We will dance for her and play cheerful music. The queen loves beautiful things around her, and we will all make sure that she has them.

Early Morning
SEVENTH MONTH. WANING MOON.

I have not had much time to write. Cleopatra is nearing the end of her pregnancy, and she has grown more demanding. She is still furious with Mark Antony and angry that she can no longer fit into her favorite clothes. Even though there are many robes that will cover her stomach, she is still irritable and fretful most of the time. It must be hard to be so heavy in this heat.

They say that the queen is having two babies, which means that Caesarion will have two little brothers or sisters—or one of each. I don't think that he will like that at all. He is used to being his mother's favorite.

Lotus is also getting heavy—that's because she is having kittens! I thought that the cooks were just giving her too many scraps again, but when I felt her belly, I could feel something moving around. I wonder how many kittens she will have.

I don't have the time to see my friends as much as I used to, and Rami only visits the palace every few days. We used to walk by the river in the evenings, but there's no time to do that nowadays. Maybe when we're married, we'll be able to. My mother tells me that Nanu and Sheriti are both going to be married next month . . . before me!

Mark Antony has not returned to Egypt, even though he knows that Cleopatra is pregnant.

Late Evening
Eighth Month. Half-Moon.

The day before yesterday, at the end of the seventh month, the queen gave birth to twins: a boy and a girl. Their names are Alexander Helios (*Helios* is the Greek word for "sun") and Cleopatra Selene (*Selene* is the Greek word for "moon"). Everyone in the palace is rejoicing. Word has been sent to Mark Antony. I wonder if he will come back to Egypt. Everyone is saying that his new wife in Rome, Octavia, will not be nearly as happy as we are here in Egypt.

Lotus has had her kittens! She is the happy mother of three lovely little ones.

Two kittens are black. The other one is exactly the same color as the amber in a bracelet that the queen gave me for cheering her up when Mark Antony went back to Rome. So that's what I've named her: Amber. The queen gives her babies to a wet nurse to be fed, but Lotus feeds her kittens herself and seems to enjoy it.

Lotus and her kittens have been shut out of the palace nursery, of course. Everyone knows that cats love to jump in infants' cradles and go to sleep among the soft blankets that are always found there—though the queen seems to love the kittens as much as she loves her babies.

In a few months I will be leaving the queen's service, because I need to return home to prepare for my marriage. I am a little nervous about this, but it will be much easier for me than for girls who hardly know their husbands when they get married. I am going to be Rami's wife. I am already good at writing, but he will be able to teach me even more.

Before the Evening Meal

Twelfth month. Full moon.

live near the palace, so we can visit there often. My cousin Iras, who is much younger than me, will take my place here soon, and when she does, I'll be able to guide her and teach her what she needs to know. I've learned so much from the queen, and even though the work has been hard, I have enjoyed being in her presence and being her Nefret, her "pretty one."

The queen called me to her chamber this morning and said, "Nefret, my pretty one, you are a woman now. You must marry and have your own children. You have been a loyal handmaid to me, but now it is time for your own life. But I have a favor to ask of you. Will you let me keep the three little cats at the palace? One for each of my children?"

How could I refuse the queen of Egypt? (I don't think that Lotus will be very happy for a while, as she will miss her little ones.)

I know that I will enjoy being Rami's wife, for we are such good friends. And we'll still

WHAT HAPPENED NEXT?

Mark Antony did not return to Alexandria for four years. He went to live in Greece with Octavia, and she had two children. Then, three years after Nefret left the palace—in the year that we now call 37 B.C.—Antony left his wife, Octavia, to return to his real love, Cleopatra. It was the first time that he had met his twin children. He married Cleopatra in an Egyptian ceremony, and they had another child, Ptolemy Philadelphus.

Now it was Octavia's turn to be furious because Antony had abandoned her and their two daughters. She went to her brother, Octavian, who persuaded the Romans to declare war on Egypt. Octavian and Antony had always been bitter rivals, so Octavian didn't hesitate.

In 31 B.C., Antony fought a sea battle against them in Actium, Greece. Cleopatra sent some ships of her own to help Antony, but the Romans won this battle. When Cleopatra saw that Antony's forces were defeated, she fled, and Antony followed her. This made the Romans think that he was unable to act on his own and was simply following where Cleopatra led him.

In 30 B.C., Octavian reached Alexandria. Cleopatra had been learning how to make poisons and experimenting to see which one would bring death most swiftly and painlessly. She had also had a huge tomblike chamber built, and when this mausoleum was ready, she moved her precious clothing, jewelry, and treasures inside it.

After another sea battle, Mark Antony was convinced that Cleopatra had betrayed him and was now on the Romans' side. She fled to her mausoleum with her maidservants Iras and Charmian, because she was sure that Mark Antony would try to kill her for what he thought was her treacherous behavior.

Cleopatra ordered her servants to tell Mark Antony that she was dead. Mark Antony believed this and begged one of his servants, Eros, to kill him. Eros killed himself instead, not wanting to harm his master. Mark Antony wept for the loss of his faithful attendant and stabbed himself with his own dagger, but he succeeded only in wounding himself very badly.

Cleopatra found out what had happened and asked to see Mark Antony. He was overjoyed that she was still alive, and he had himself taken to the mausoleum. He was hauled up through the window because the door was locked against the Romans. Cleopatra was distraught when she saw that her beloved Mark Antony was dying. She laid him on her own bed and called him her husband and lord. Mark Antony died, asking her to remember only the happy times that they had shared.

Octavian allowed Cleopatra to arrange Mark Antony's funeral. She buried him with royal splendor and then retired to her bed, saying that she wanted nothing more than to join him in death. Octavian guarded her very closely, fearing that she intended to take her own life, but in the end Cleopatra persuaded him that she was feeling better and could be allowed to return to the mausoleum.

Once she was safely back among her own servants, Cleopatra took a bath and ordered a feast. While this was being prepared, a man arrived at the gate with a basket of figs. Cleopatra's guards checked the basket and found nothing suspicious in it. After the feast, the queen wrote a letter to Octavian, sealed it, and sent a messenger to deliver it to him. The letter asked Octavian to allow her to be buried in Mark Antony's tomb. Octavian realized that this meant that Cleopatra intended to kill herself, and he sent soldiers to the mausoleum at once. They arrived too late. Cleopatra was dead on her bed. The soldiers found two pinpricks on the queen's arm, and a story developed that she had allowed herself to be bitten by an asp, an extremely poisonous snake, that had been hidden inside the basket of figs all along. She was buried, as she had wished, beside her beloved Mark Antony.

Cleopatra's Family Tree

Cleopatra was a member of the Ptolemy family. The first Ptolemy was Macedonian and one of Alexander the Great's generals. When Alexander died in 323 B.C., Ptolemy decided that he would be the ruler of Egypt and become Ptolemy I. Instead of being a soldier, he would become a god-king.

But because Ptolemy was a god-king, he could not marry an ordinary woman—he had to marry a member of his own family. That is why all of the Ptolemies married their sisters (or, in Cleopatra's case, her brothers). The children of the Ptolemies were all named Ptolemy or Cleopatra (except for Cleopatra's children, but that's because they had Roman fathers rather than Ptolemy fathers).

Cleopatra was the last queen of Egypt. After her death, Egypt became a Roman province. Her son Caesarion was murdered by his own tutor on Octavian's orders. Octavian was worried that Caesarion might grow up to be a threat because he was Julius Caesar's son. Cleopatra's other three children were sent to Rome, where they were raised by Octavia, Mark Antony's Roman widow.

Cleopatra's son Caesarion was murdered on Octavian's orders.

NEFRET'S WORLD

Although Nefret's diary is a story, the places, people, and events that she writes about are real. Egypt was one of the most famous civilizations of the ancient world, and it had been in existence for almost 4,000 years before Nefret was born. The pyramids and great temples had been built around 3,000 years earlier, so, for Nefret, they were ancient history.

For its final 1,000 years, Egypt was conquered in turn by different peoples: the Assyrians, the Parthians, the Greeks, and the Romans. Nefret lived to see the end of the ancient Egyptian era.

Alexandria was not founded until 331 B.C.—that is why it does not appear on this older map. The city was located on the coast.

MAP KEY
- ■ capital city
- • other city, town, or village
- ▲ pyramid

3500 B.C.
3500 Farming flourishes in the Nile river valley

3300 First Egyptian towns built
3300–3000 Hieroglyphic writing is developed

3000 B.C.
3000 Upper and Lower Egypt united, with capital in Memphis
2920 First dynasty of kings begins to rule
2630 First step pyramid built in Saqqara
2575 Sneferu founds IV Dynasty and establishes powerful Old Kingdom based in Memphis
2550 Khufu (Cheops) builds Great Pyramid in Giza

2500 B.C.

2134 Old Kingdom ends as Egypt divides into two rival kingdoms
2040 Egypt reunified under XI Dynasty, establishing the Middle Kingdom

2000 B.C.
1640–1550 Hyksos people from the Levant conquer and rule Lower Egypt

1550 Ahmose founds XVIII Dynasty and establishes New Kingdom

1500 B.C.
1473–1458 Hatshepsut is the queen and sends naval expedition to Punt in east Africa
1353–1335 Akhenaton creates a short-lived monotheistic (one-god) religion based on Aton, the sun god
1333–1323 Reign of Tutankhamen, the boy pharaoh
1290–1224 Rameses II extends Egyptian Empire into the Levant
1070 Fall of XXI Dynasty marks end of effective Egyptian power
1000 B.C.

671–651 Assyrians occupy Egypt

525–523 Persians briefly conquer Egypt

500 B.C.
332 Alexander the Great conquers Egypt, establishing a new Ptolemaic Dynasty

30 Death of Cleopatra, the last Egyptian pharaoh; Egypt becomes part of the Roman Empire

0

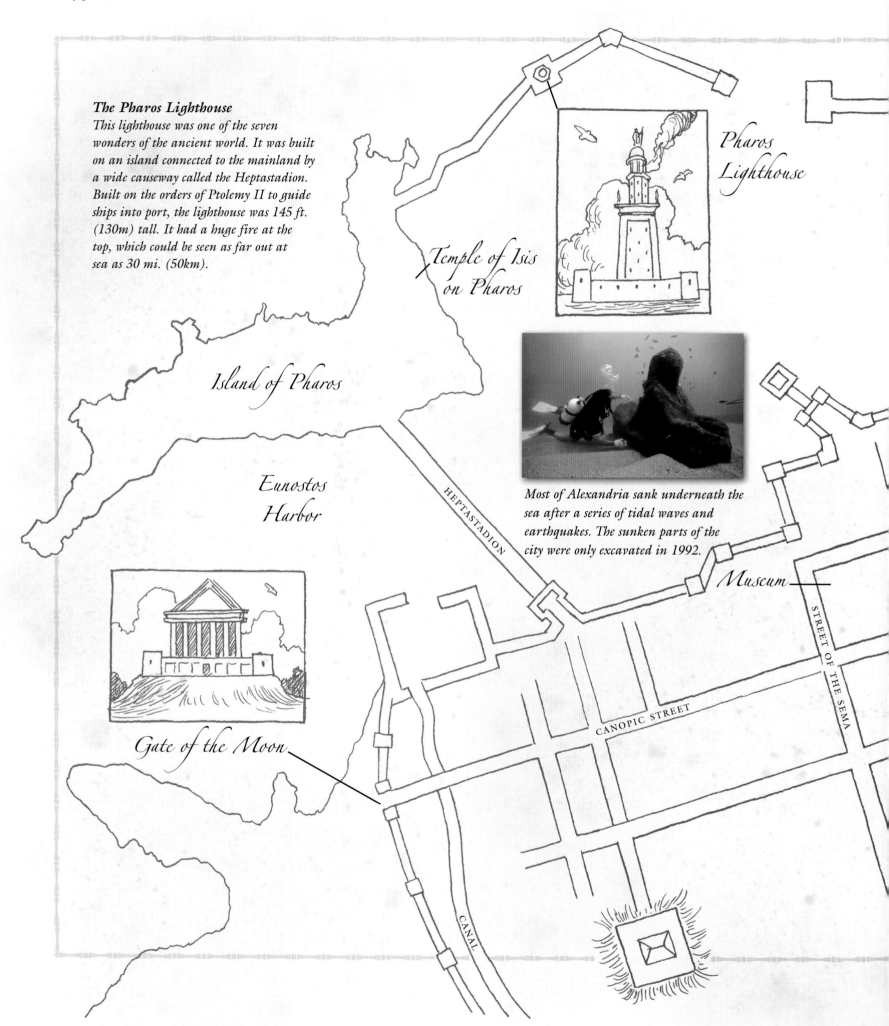

The Pharos Lighthouse
This lighthouse was one of the seven wonders of the ancient world. It was built on an island connected to the mainland by a wide causeway called the Heptastadion. Built on the orders of Ptolemy II to guide ships into port, the lighthouse was 145 ft. (130m) tall. It had a huge fire at the top, which could be seen as far out at sea as 30 mi. (50km).

Temple of Isis on Pharos

Pharos Lighthouse

Island of Pharos

Eunostos Harbor

HEPTASTADION

Most of Alexandria sank underneath the sea after a series of tidal waves and earthquakes. The sunken parts of the city were only excavated in 1992.

Museum

STREET OF THE SEMA

Gate of the Moon

CANOPIC STREET

CANAL

Probable palace site

The Royal Palace
*Alexandria was laid out
as a grid. The royal palace
was in the northeast part of
the city, in an area called
the Brucheion, overlooking
the sea. This area is now
underwater; the land
was swallowed up by
the sea hundreds of
years later.*

*Gate of
the Sun*

CANAL

The Library and the Museum
*Alexandria was a place for entertainment
and learning. Ptolemy I founded the famous
library that, during Cleopatra's time, had
around 700,000 works in it.*

*The museum was a center for learning, and
many people would gather there to study and
to discuss astronomy, math, philosophy, and
other subjects.*

The Market
*This was always full of produce—exotic fruit,
foodstuffs, spices, and wines—as well as ivory,
crafts, cloth, and toys.*

ALEXANDRIA

At the time of Cleopatra's reign, Alexandria was the largest city
in the ancient world. It started out as a little village on the sea
called Ra-Kedet. Then Alexander the Great—the Greek general
who had conquered Egypt in 332 B.C.—decided to build a large
city there. The city was founded in 331 B.C., and Alexander
named it after himself, but he never had a chance to live there.
Having left Egypt to fight more battles, Alexander died at the
age of 33. His body was returned to Alexandria, and the city
became the new capital of ancient Egypt. With its position
at the mouth of the Nile delta, it was perfectly placed at the
crossroad of Europe, Africa, and Asia. By the time that
Cleopatra was born, Alexandria had monuments, palaces,
theaters, temples, and a museum and a library.

Today nothing survives from Alexander the Great's original
city. Egypt's capital city, Cairo, was founded 1,000 years later.

THE PEOPLE

Alexandria was a crowded city with many different communities. Three main groups of people lived there: the Greeks who lived in the center of the city; the Jews who lived in the east of the city; and the Egyptians—the poorest group—who lived in the old city in the west. There were also thousands of travelers who passed through Alexandria; there were traders and camel caravans from Africa and Asia and seafarers from all over the world, bringing goods and armies to Egypt.

Linen is made from a plant called flax. The Egyptians spun and wove it into lengths of light cloth for clothing.

Hair

Hairstyles were very important to girls and women in ancient Egypt. They wore their hair in different ways: long, curly, crimped, or braided and decorated with ribbons and flowers. Young servant girls would often wear their hair in thin braids, with fragrant incense cones on their heads. These would melt slowly in the heat, and a wonderful scent would surround them.

Clothing

Clothes were very simple, and young children were often naked. Girls and women from richer families wore clothing made from white linen, which became finer and more see-through over the years. Their outer garments were often pleated, and belts, jewelry, and thin shawls were often worn to add color. Jewelry was not just for wealthy women—wealthy men wore plenty too.

Beauty and makeup

Because Egypt was a hot and dry country, the ancient Egyptians had to use plenty of moisturizer to keep their skin feeling soft. The poor used castor oil, but the rich used scented oils that often took around six months to produce. Fresh incense under the arms was an effective ancient Egyptian deodorant. Men *and* women wore makeup. Eyes had to be large and almond-shaped, with different colors being fashionable at different times.

Young boys and girls wore their hair in a "side lock of youth" until they were around ten years old.

THE ROMAN ARMY

During Cleopatra's reign, there were many Roman soldiers living in Alexandria. Julius Caesar left behind three legions of them to look after her when he returned to Rome. Each legion was made up of infantrymen called legionaries; the soldiers in charge of them, called centurions; and the generals in charge of each legion. There was also the cavalry, who were soldiers on horseback, and auxiliaries—neither of these two divisions were Roman citizens.

Soldiers were trained to fight together. They marched into battle in a line with their shields next to each other. If the enemy shot arrows at them, the soldiers in the rows behind the front line would lift up their shields over their heads like a roof to protect them. This was called a testudo, which means "tortoise."

Life for Roman soldiers away from home could be very lonely. Some mothers would send their sons letters and packages from Italy to stop them from feeling so homesick!

Mark Antony's army went into battle against Octavian with as many as 75,000 legionaries, 25,000 auxiliaries, and 12,000 cavalry in it.

To show the difference in rank, some centurions carried a stick with which they beat any soldier who disobeyed an order. The important centurions also wore special armor, which emphasized their rank.

auxiliary

general

legionary

centurion

cavalry

The Nile River

The Nile river flows right through the middle of Egypt. Starting from the mountains of central Africa, the river runs all the way to the Mediterranean Sea. When the snow melts in the mountains, the river flows faster. Every spring the Nile used to flood (before the Aswan High Dam was completed in the 1970s), with the water spreading for miles. When the floodwater drained away, it left behind rich, fertile soil.

Farming

Farmers dug canals in order to take the water from the river to their crops. They grew grain to make bread, flax to make cloth, grapes to make wine, as well as other fruit and vegetables. Their cattle would graze on the land, and from them they would get meat, milk, and leather—they had everything that they needed. But this depended on the river flooding each year. If it didn't, there was a drought year, meaning that there was no harvest and, therefore, no food.

Food

The Egyptians liked to eat three times each day. The morning meal was called "mouthwashing," and it was usually eaten alone. The afternoon and evening meals, called "the rising of the stars," were eaten with family and friends. Tomb paintings show that Egyptians ate all types of fruit, vegetables, meat, and fish. They baked 35 different types of breads and cakes. Ordinary Egyptians drank a thick beer made from grain. The beer was brewed at home. Richer people drank sweet wine that was served in jugs.

Papyrus

Nefret tells us that she wrote on rolls of papyrus. Papyrus is a plant that grew in the marshes around the Nile river, and the thick stems were used to make many things: ropes, baskets, and sometimes even boats. But, most importantly, they were used to make a type of writing material. The stems were cut into strips, and the strips were laid on top of each other to make sheets. One scroll was called a papyrus; two or more scrolls were called papyruses. The sheets—usually in squares—were attached together to make a roll. If you were poor, you would write on both sides.

The calendar

The earliest Egyptian calendar was based on the annual flooding of the Nile river. The Egyptians divided the year into 12 months and three seasons: akhet (the flooding), peret (the spring, when the crops grew), and shemu (harvest time). Each season consisted of four 30-day months, and each month had three ten-day weeks. Day and night were divided into 12 hours each.

During Nefret's time, Julius Caesar made changes to the calendar, and the Julian calendar was developed, which is the basis of our modern calendar.

Papyrus was a precious resource, and the ancient Egyptians knew how to recycle it. Many surviving letters written on papyrus were "palimpset"—that is, written on top of an earlier letter.

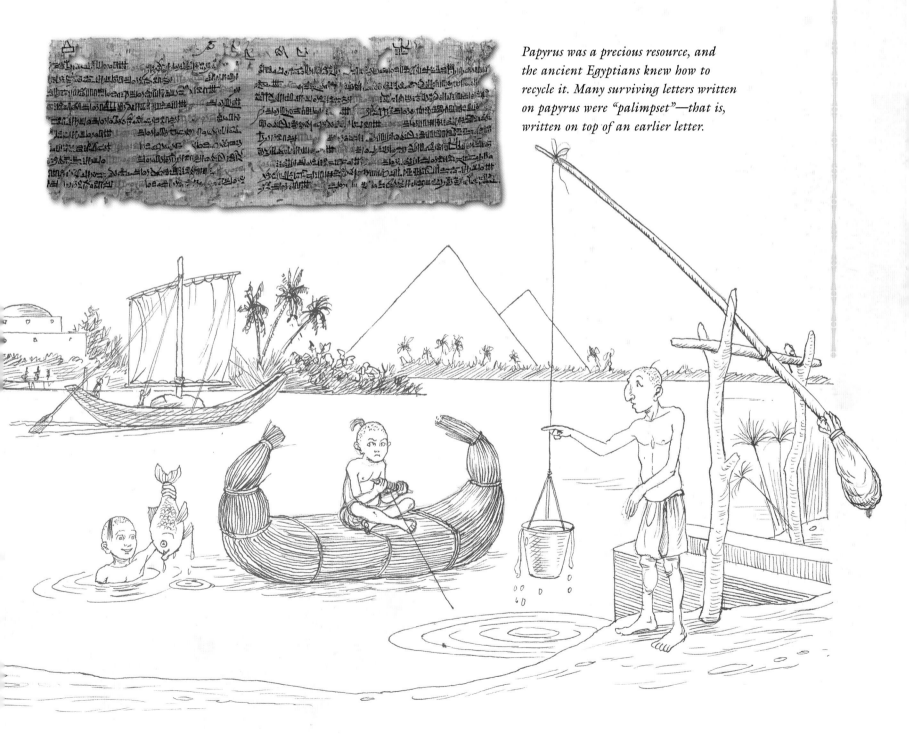

CHILDREN AND EDUCATION

Nefret tells us that she had older brothers and a little sister, Kebi. Most families in ancient Egypt had four or five children who lived beyond adolescence. They would also have had more babies who died during childbirth or shortly after.

There were more than 3,000 hieroglyphic signs, and 800 were used regularly. To become a scribe, you would have had to learn at least 700 hieroglyphs.

Most children in ancient Egypt—and the majority of Egyptian adults—could not read or write. Boys learned the trades of their fathers and took over from them when they could no longer work. Boys from the upper classes of Egyptian society learned how to read and write and also learned mathematics. These boys would probably have been taught in scribal schools attached to a temple or a palace.

Girls learned domestic skills, like cooking and weaving, from their mothers. They had no formal education and were unlikely to be able to read and write. There were exceptions, however, as we have found letters written by women. Some, like Nefret, may have learned this skill from a scribe who was a family friend.

Learning was by rote—repeating things over and over again until they were memorized. The teachers were very strict. One surviving text says, "A boy's ear is on his back—he listens when he is beaten."

Writing

Nefret was very lucky to have a friend like Rami to teach her how to write, because it was very unusual for girls in ancient Egypt to be able to do this. Most people think of hieroglyphics when they think of ancient Egyptian writing. But this form of writing had virtually died out by Cleopatra's time, except for religious carvings and the official writing of the royal name. Nonreligious writing on papyrus scrolls used demotic script.

A reed pen was made by cutting and shaping a single reed straw or length of bamboo. They were the most common writing implements during Cleopatra's time. A scribe kept his pens in a palette made from wood or ivory.

The text on the Rosetta stone (now on display in the British Museum in London, England)— dated March 27, 196 B.C.—tells of the good things that Ptolemy V had done for Egypt.

The Rosetta stone

This shows the same piece of writing in hieroglyphic, demotic, and Greek scripts. It was only when this stone was discovered in A.D. 1799 in the village of el-Rashid (Rosetta) that Egyptologists were able to begin to decipher Egyptian hieroglyphics. The names of Ptolemy and Cleopatra were deciphered on the stone first. Later—in A.D. 1822—these words provided the Egyptologist Jean François Champollion with the means to understand hieroglyphics.

PHARAOHS, PYRAMIDS, AND RELIGION

Pharaohs were the rulers of ancient Egypt—the kings and queens. The word comes from *per-aa*, meaning "great house," and describes the royal court rather than the person. The Egyptians believed that their rulers were gods or children of gods. Cleopatra thought of herself as the goddess Isis. She was the last queen of ancient Egypt.

Pharaohs wore several different crowns to symbolize their many roles in Egyptian society.

In Egyptian temples, Cleopatra (below) had herself portrayed with all of the attributes of a pharaoh, but as the goddess Isis come down to Earth.

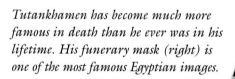

Tutankhamen has become much more famous in death than he ever was in his lifetime. His funerary mask (right) is one of the most famous Egyptian images.

Two famous pharaohs

Tutankhamen was the pharaoh between 1336–1327 B.C. He was only around eight years old when he became the ruler of ancient Egypt. His tomb was discovered in the Valley of the Kings in A.D. 1922.

Hatshepsut was a famous female pharaoh who ruled from around 1479–1458 B.C. She is known as "the woman who reigned as a man" and is often depicted with a royal beard. She had a tomb built in the Valley of the Kings, but was never buried there.

The Valley of the Kings

This was the main royal cemetery of ancient Egypt. There are 62 tombs there. The smallest tomb in the valley is Tutankhamen's. The valley had stopped being used well before the Ptolemies ruled Egypt. Cleopatra was buried with Mark Antony, but their tomb has never been found.

Pyramids were built high to help the pharaoh's spirit rise to the stars. They were constructed from stone in order to protect the pharaoh's embalmed body and to house his or her precious belongings, needed for the afterlife. There were two types—the "step pyramid" (above) and the "true pyramid" (below).

The Great Pyramid in Giza is the largest surviving pyramid. It was built by Khufu (Cheops), the son of Sneferu.

GODS AND GODDESSES

In temple carvings and paintings, statues, and mummy cases, the gods are shown in different forms. Sometimes they appear as humans, sometimes as humans with the heads of animals or birds, and sometimes solely as animals. The Egyptians had hundreds of gods and goddesses.

The major gods and goddesses

Osiris is the ruler of the underworld. He is usually shown wrapped as a mummy, but with his hands projecting from the cloths in order to hold the royal crook and flail. He wears a tall white crown with feathers on both sides and sometimes with the horns of a ram. Osiris was killed by his jealous brother, Seth.

Re (or Ra) is the sun god and "father" of all pharaohs. He is usually depicted with a human body and a falcon's head, on which is a sun and a sacred asp.

Isis is the sister and wife of Osiris. The goddess of the harvest, Isis is usually depicted with a horn and a sun on her head and wearing beautiful robes. Cleopatra thought of herself as Isis and loved dressing up as her.

Seth is the god of chaos and destruction and the evil brother of Osiris. Seth is generally shown with a human body, but with the head of an animal a little like an anteater. But sometimes he's been represented as a hippopotamus, a pig, or a donkey. Seth locked Osiris in a coffin and threw him into the Nile river. Isis found the coffin, but so did Seth, who then made sure that he was really dead by chopping him up into small pieces.

Horus is the son of Isis. He is sometimes depicted as a falcon and sometimes as a man with a falcon's head (like Re). Horus was the god of the sky. In Cleopatra's time, a new image of Horus emerged, and small sculptures in wood and stone have been found showing Horus as a naked child-god standing on a crocodile or holding poisonous snakes.

The afterlife

The ancient Egyptians did not believe that death was the end of a person's life. People who died needed their bodies so that their spirit, the ka, could return to them after the funeral service.

Mummies

In order to preserve a body, the Egyptian embalmers mummified it. The best way of preserving a body was to remove all of the internal organs and then clean out the inside with wine and spices. Then the body was covered with embalming agents for at least 40 days in order to mummify it. After this time the body was wrapped from head to toe in cloth that was soaked in a type of glue.

Egyptians believed that the journey to the next world should be as smooth as possible. Amulets, such as this one, were bound inside the mummy's layers of linen for good luck.

Mummy cases

The embalmers would give the prepared body back to the relatives, who would place it in a decorated wooden coffin—a mummy case that was shaped like the dead person. The relatives would place the mummy, upright, in a burial chamber, together with the person's favorite possessions for life after death.

Mummification was only for the rich—poorer people were buried in simple graves in the sand, allowing the bodies to be preserved naturally.

GLOSSARY

Alexander the Great
The king of Macedonia, from 336–323 B.C., who conquered many lands and is the hero in many ancient Greek legends.

allies
Countries that are friends or joined by an agreement called a treaty.

Aphrodite
The ancient Greek goddess of love and beauty.

asp
A poisonous snake, such as the Egyptian cobra, that was a symbol of royalty in ancient Egypt.

astrology
The study of the impact of the stars and planets on people's lives.

chamber
A room, especially a bedroom.

charms
Ornaments that are worn because people believe that they bring good luck or ward off evil.

civil war
A war between people who live in the same country.

Cleopatra
(69–30 B.C.) There were a number of Egyptian queens named Cleopatra, but the most famous was Cleopatra VII (the Cleopatra who features in this book). She was a lover of Julius Caesar and Mark Antony. She became the queen upon the death of her father in 51 B.C. and ruled Egypt with her two brother-husbands, Ptolemy XIII and Ptolemy XIV, and then with her son Ptolemy XV Caesar (Caesarion).

Cupid
The ancient Roman god of love.

delta
A triangular area at the mouth of a river where sediment is deposited.

demotic script
A type of ancient Egyptian writing that came after the picture writing called hieroglyphics.

enchantress
A woman who puts charms or spells on people.

flood
When a river overflows its banks onto land that is normally dry.

fragrant
Having a sweet smell.

gemstones
Precious stones that are used in jewelry.

generals
The top officers in an army.

grain
Wheat, barley, or oats.

handmaid
A female servant or personal maid.

harvest
The time of gathering ripe crops.

headdress
A decorative head covering.

hieroglyphics
A system of picture writing used by the ancient Egyptians.

Horus
An ancient Egyptian god in the form of a falcon.

Isis
An ancient Egyptian goddess who was the sister-wife of Osiris and the mother of Horus.

jetty
A landing platform by the side of a river.

Julius Caesar (100–44 B.C.) A Roman general and emperor who was assassinated on the Ides of March (March 15) in 44 B.C.

kohl
A mixture of soot and other ingredients used to darken the eyelids and eyelashes.

legion
A unit of the ancient Roman army made up of between 3,000 and 6,000 soldiers.

Mark Antony (83–30 B.C.) A Roman general who served under Julius Caesar and later ruled Rome along with Octavian and Lepidus. He was defeated by Octavian (the future Emperor Augustus) and committed suicide with Cleopatra in 30 B.C.

mausoleum
A tomb above the ground.

merchant traders
People who buy and sell things for profit.

papyrus
An ancient Egyptian paper made from reeds.

plains
Large areas of flat land.

plotting
Secretly planning.

Pompey (106–48 B.C.) A Roman general and politician who led Rome with Julius Caesar and Marcus Crassus between

61–54 B.C. He was later defeated in battle by Caesar and murdered by Ptolemy XIII.

port
A harbor or a town with a harbor.

Ptolemy XIII (63–47 B.C.) A younger brother of Cleopatra VII, who became the joint ruler of Egypt with her after their father's death. He died as he tried to flee from Caesar's forces in 47 B.C.

Ptolemy XIV (59–44 B.C.) A younger brother of Cleopatra VII, who coruled Egypt with his sister until he was killed in order to make way for her son by Julius Caesar, Ptolemy XV Caesar (Caesarion).

Roman Empire
An ancient state centered around the city of Rome, which was ruled by emperors until its collapse in A.D. 476.

Roman province
The Roman Empire was divided into provinces, which

were governed by Roman officials.

rushlights
Candles with wicks made from plants called rushes.

salve
A soothing substance applied to wounds.

sandalwood
A type of tree that has scented wood.

scribes
People in ancient Egyptian times whose job involved reading and writing.

scroll
A roll of papyrus used for writing.

starve
To suffer from hunger.

stern
The back part of a ship.

Tarsus
An ancient city in modern-day Turkey that was part of the Roman Empire during Cleopatra's lifetime.

temples
Buildings in which people pray and worship.

washerwomen
Women who wash clothes.

wet nurse
A woman who cares for and breastfeeds children who are not her own.

INDEX

ACKNOWLEDGMENTS

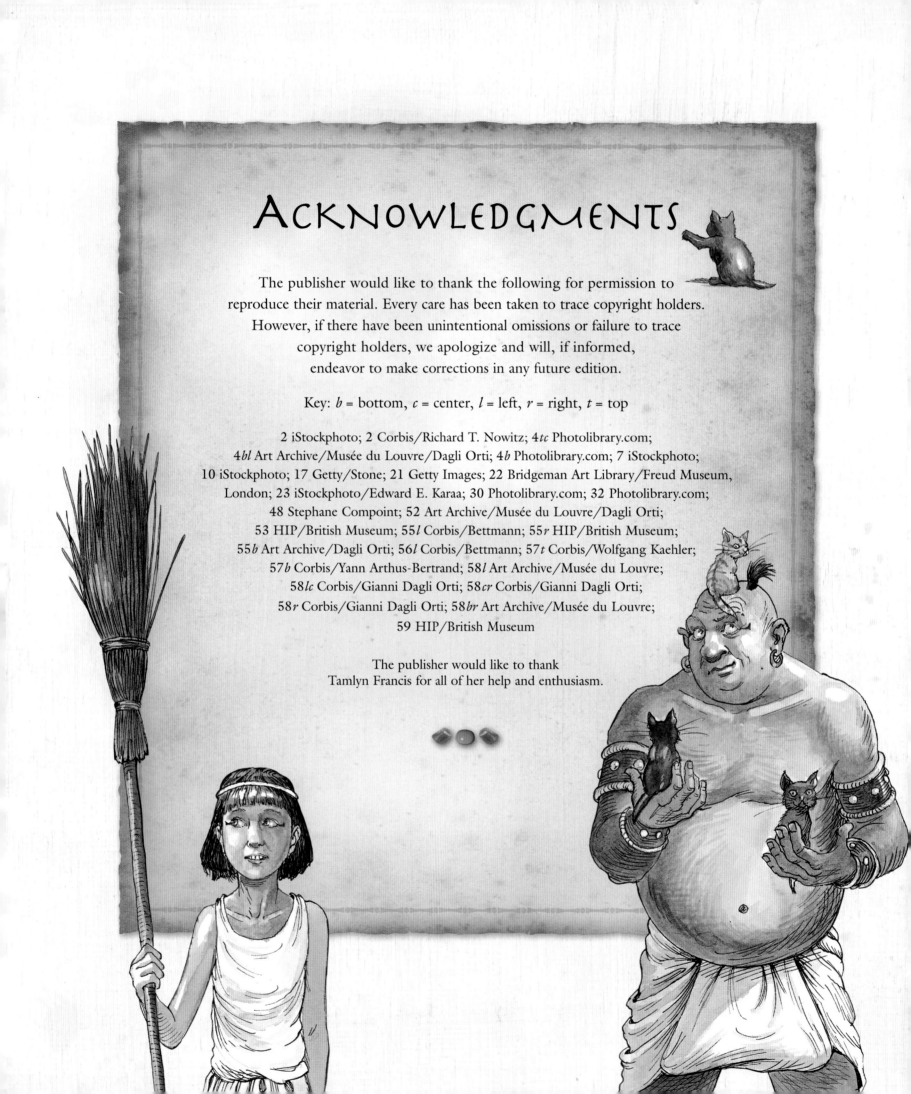

The publisher would like to thank the following for permission to
reproduce their material. Every care has been taken to trace copyright holders.
However, if there have been unintentional omissions or failure to trace
copyright holders, we apologize and will, if informed,
endeavor to make corrections in any future edition.

Key: *b* = bottom, *c* = center, *l* = left, *r* = right, *t* = top

2 iStockphoto; 2 Corbis/Richard T. Nowitz; 4*tc* Photolibrary.com;
4*bl* Art Archive/Musée du Louvre/Dagli Orti; 4*b* Photolibrary.com; 7 iStockphoto;
10 iStockphoto; 17 Getty/Stone; 21 Getty Images; 22 Bridgeman Art Library/Freud Museum,
London; 23 iStockphoto/Edward E. Karaa; 30 Photolibrary.com; 32 Photolibrary.com;
48 Stephane Compoint; 52 Art Archive/Musée du Louvre/Dagli Orti;
53 HIP/British Museum; 55*l* Corbis/Bettmann; 55*r* HIP/British Museum;
55*b* Art Archive/Dagli Orti; 56*l* Corbis/Bettmann; 57*t* Corbis/Wolfgang Kaehler;
57*b* Corbis/Yann Arthus-Bertrand; 58*l* Art Archive/Musée du Louvre;
58*lc* Corbis/Gianni Dagli Orti; 58*cr* Corbis/Gianni Dagli Orti;
58*r* Corbis/Gianni Dagli Orti; 58*br* Art Archive/Musée du Louvre;
59 HIP/British Museum

The publisher would like to thank
Tamlyn Francis for all of her help and enthusiasm.